On My
Papa's Shoulders

CATALYST PRESS
El Paso, Texas

For fathers and sons

Text and illustrations copyright © Niki Daly 2022

For further information, write Catalyst Press at info@catalystpress.org

In North America, this book is published by Catalyst Press and distributed
by Consortium Book Sales & Distribution, a division of Ingram.
Phone: 612/746-2600
cbsdinfo@ingramcontent.com
www.cbsd.com

First published in Great Britain in 2022 by Otter-Barry Books,
Little Orchard, Burley Gate, Herefordshire, HR1 3QS
www.otterbarrybooks.com

Illustrated with mixed media
Set in Maiandra GD
Printed in China

FIRST EDITION
10 9 8 7 6 5 4 3 2 1
Library of Congress Control Number: 2021952181

On My Papa's Shoulders

Niki Daly

Most days I walk to school with Mama.
She holds my hand tightly
and we walk quickly along the busy road.

Cars toot and zoom,
feet tap-tap,
people chat-chat.

And sometimes I have to stop
for Mama to help tie my shoe laces.

"Let's hurry and beat the school bell!" says Mama.

We always do and still have time to kiss
and say goodbye.

"Have a happy day," Mama always calls
as I run through the school gate.

Some days Gogo takes me to school.
We always leave early so that we don't have to hurry.
Gogo doesn't like the busy road so we go the quiet way.

We walk, look, and talk-talk.

"Look, a hungry cat."

Gogo lets me share some of my lunch
with him.

Then we walk on and talk some more.

"Tell me about your friends."

I tell her about my best friends Jake, Ben and Boo.

"We must hold our friends gently in both hands," says Gogo.

Gogo is wise. Her hands are old and gentle. She lets go of my hand so that I can run ahead and join my friends, Jake, Ben and Boo, waiting for me at school.

On days when it's cold and rainy
Tata likes to take me to school.

We splash in puddles
as we go along wet back-streets,
through a soggy park,
under dripping trees.

Tata knows all the shortcuts.

But he always has to rest for a while.
Then he's ready to whistle again. Tata is a great whistler.
His favourite tune is, *Don't Worry Be Happy*.
And off we go!

I run ahead of Tata, then stop and look back,
just to make sure he's still behind me.

Tata never holds my hand
but he's a great hugger.
I always get a BIG hug
when he catches up
at the school gate.

But the days I love the best
are when Papa takes me to school.

Papa is strong and tall.
When he lifts me onto his shoulders
I'm as high as a cloud and can see the whole world.

Papa asks, "How are you doing up there, my boy?"

I pat his head and say, "Fine, thanks."

I want to stay on Papa's shoulders for ever and ever.

But here's the school and it's time to
come down and say goodbye.

Papa kneels beside me,
puts his hands on my shoulders,
looks me in the eye and says,
"I love you."

"I love you too," I say.

That's how we like to say goodbye
when Papa goes to work...

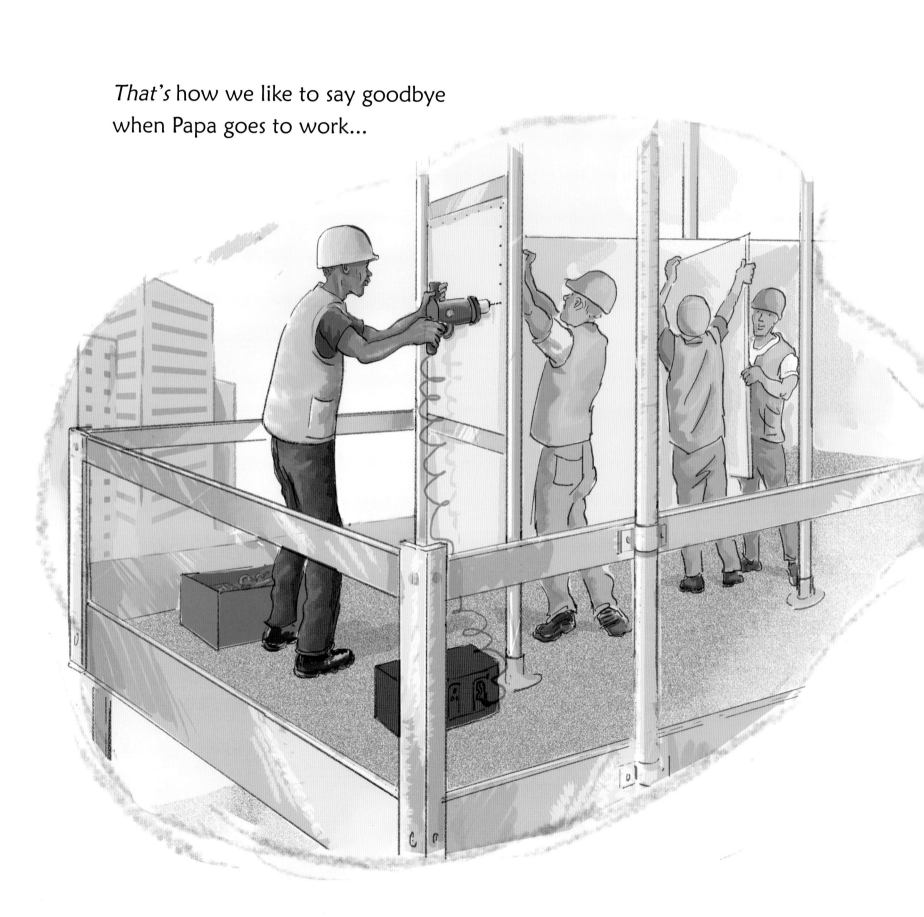

and I go to school.